Suffolk Pride:

We are the One in Five

Queer stories inspired by Gilbert Baker's Pride flag.

Forewords by Simon James Green and The Gilbert Baker Foundation

First edition 2023

Edited by Charlie Brodie

Cover design and illustrations by Laura Ayers

Published by Suffolk Queer Voices

Printed and bound in Great Britain by Clays Ltd, Elcograf
S.p.A
ISBN: 978-1-7395613-0-7

For Gilbert Baker and all the queer people who are on the journey of discovering their sexuality, gender, and identity. Have pride and be strong.

'The rainbow is a part of nature, and you have to be in the right place to see it. It's beautiful, all of the colors, even the colors you can't see. That really fit us as a people because we are all of the colors. We are all the genders, races, and ages.'

– Gilbert Baker

Introduction

This is a student led anthology of Suffolk queer voices, showcasing short prose, poetry and non-fiction writing from undergraduate, postgraduate, and alumni students of UOS, with a special addition from Ashley Hickson-Lovence. The project is sympathetic to the Own Voices movement, being written, edited, and curated by the queer community or individuals with queer lived experience (whether personal or familial). The anthology hopes to shed a positive light onto rural communities and their connections to queerness such as Suffolk, sitting in contrast to other queer anthologised works which have a national or international focus. This work promotes the underrepresented rural experience of queerness, exploring themes of isolation, identity and otherness within fictional works written by queer writers in Suffolk.

Whilst a number of queer anthologies have been published in recent years, none have been produced by local competing institutions within East Anglia. Queer voices from within rural communities are an underrepresented demographic in publications, and this anthology seeks to address this disparity, creating a platform for these overlooked and underrepresented voices.

The project commemorates the 45th anniversary of Gilbert Baker's Pride flag which utilised the rainbow as a symbol of unity. Baker allocated a meaning for each colour that was representative of the community, and which will be represented within the structure and themes of this collection.

It also marks the 20th anniversary of the repeal of Section 28, a conservative legislation that banned the promotion of queer work within academic institutions. Our anthology pushes back against this repealed legislation highlighting the acceptance and diversity that is present within these institutions now.

We hope that you can find comfort, solace, and a place of acceptance here within this book.

Foreword by Simon James Green, author of *Boy Like Me*

I grew up in a small town in the middle of rural Lincolnshire. It was the mid-90s, so the section 28 legislation which banned LGBTQ+ books from school libraries was in full force. It also meant anything to do with being LGBTQ+ was never discussed in classes. It was as if we just didn't exist... with the exception of hurtful slurs in the playground, of course – it was always OK to talk about gay people if it was being said in a hateful, disparaging way. If you wanted any queer representation, you had to head to a dark corner of the bookshop with the shelves labelled 'Gay & Lesbian' (other identities clearly not existing). Doing that always felt shameful. What if someone you knew saw you? How would you explain it?

While I'll always be grateful to those books for how they helped me start to figure myself out as a teenager, one thing stood out in most of the narratives: queer folk might exist in rural communities, but to truly live as their authentic selves, they always had to move to the big city. Under the bright lights, on the bustling pavements and in the buzzing clubs – that's where these outcasts, shunned by their small-minded families and neighbours, really found themselves, lived, and *shone*.

Clearly, I was going to have to leave Lincolnshire.

It's easy to see how those stories came about. Pre-social media, pre-internet, in a world that was even less accepting than it is now, the isolation was real because there was no visibility. I didn't know of anyone in my small town who was LGBT. Not a single soul. Being 'gay' (other identities clearly didn't exist!) was only even spoken about in the most hurtful of ways. *Dirty. Disgusting. Depraved.* The tabloids screamed hate almost every day. The AIDS epidemic was terrifying. There was ignorance, and there was fear, and worst of all, there was no one else like me. But apparently there was… in cities like London, New York and San Francisco.

How life-changing it might have been, then, had I been able to pick up an anthology like this. How heart-swellingly beautiful it would have been to have realised how so many queer experiences *do* exist, how so many queer people live and thrive, away from the major towns and cities. *Right here!* In the sort of place I was growing up.

Visibility matters. If you never see people like you, in your circumstances, living your sort of life in the sort of place you live, you think you're the only one. You become afraid. You try to deny who you really are, because standing out and being different makes you feel so vulnerable. But why should anyone feel like they have to leave their roots, the place they love, or somewhere they long to be, because they feel so alone? This beautiful, inspirational, and moving anthology is a testament to the fact there is no one way to be queer, and no one geographical location where the queer community exists. It's a loud and proud call to be seen by a world that often overlooks the rural experience in favour of what is perceived to be a more aspirational and glamorous urban existence. And it's a lifeline both for those unable to be their true selves, as well as a new generation, telling them they're OK, they're not alone, there are others just like them. Right here. In the place they call home.

One thing that struck me, reading through these stories and poems, was how progress is so slow. How some things don't ever change. One theme that crops up time and again here is a lack of acceptance, or, at least, a very real fear of that. In recent years, it feels like we've gone backwards. From the LGBTQ+ book bans in the US to the virulently transphobic rhetoric in the UK media, and the horrific lurch to the far right so many politicians have taken, the world seems to be full of people who won't ever accept us. But worse, they often make no secret of their desire to destroy us. Unwilling to listen, understand or empathise, fuelled by culture war lies, and perfectly happy mired in their own ignorance and hate, they want us to disappear, be quiet, unseen.

Visibility matters.

When they want to silence us, we have to speak louder. When they want to intimidate us, we stand together, resolute and brave. When they trade in hate, fear and shame, we counter that with love, light and pride. Every single one of the pieces in this anthology does that. The tales of struggle gives us courage for the fight. The tales of love give us hope. And all of them remind us that this world is for everyone, and we're all allowed to be who we are, and love who we love, without fear and without judgement.

Thank you and congratulations to every writer who has contributed to Suffolk Pride: We are the One in Five. Putting your stories out there, being visible, takes courage. I hope this book finds its way into the hands of the many readers who need it, who will get to see themselves and feel the warm comfort of finally realising they're not alone, there are many of us, and we'll continue to fight for a kinder, fairer, more loving world. Together, friends. Always together.

Simon James Green

Foreword by Charles Beal
President of the Gilbert Baker Foundation

Color is a human concept, created by the ancient Greeks. Research shows that early civilizations didn't conceive of colors until around the fourth century BC when the color red was first found in early literature to describe blood in a battle. Then the color blue appeared describing the sea and sky, then yellow for a flower and so on and so forth.

The point is that color is what you make it, and different colors mean different things to different people and societies. At the Gilbert Baker Foundation we think of colors in a very special way. When Gilbert Baker and his happy band of volunteers created the first Rainbow Flags in 1978, they did not see our community divided into colors. There was no "L" stripe or "G" stripe or "B" stripe or "T" stripe sewn into their flag. Baker decided to assign human elements to each color in the flag. Elements in all of us, because Gilbert saw our community as unified, "the Rainbow of Humanity." He wanted the flag to be a living, evolving work of art that would change and grow as our community grew along with it.

In this edition of Suffolk Queer Voices, we see the full spectrum of our collective humanity amplified in ways both comforting and provocative, as a group and as individuals. The full spectrum of our humanity is explored in the short stories and poetry in these pages.

Like the Original Rainbow flag, this edition of Suffolk Queer Voices is divided into 8 sections representing the 8 original colors of Baker's flag.

Pink is for sex. It is also the pink triangle created by the Nazis, signifying the status of a queer prisoner bound for the gas chambers. And the pink triangle is also from ACT-UP so it can signify defiance and victory over adversity. Pink is also the impending sex of a honeymoon for newlyweds, and the discovery of the possibility of sex by a young girl who might be a lesbian and might have met her first girlfriend.

Red is for Life. In these pages, it is also a metaphor for how neurodivergence and queerness become pathways to an authentic life. The more authentic the life, the redder it is. Our sexuality and neurologies are on a spectrum, in this case it moves from a dull gray to a vivid red. An authentic life is a life lived vividly!

Orange is for Healing. It signifies the struggle that is healing, both physically and mentally. Compassion, kindness, happiness and safety are a recipe and balm for healing an identity that has been distorted into pain by societal expectations. In this volume, we find that healing is a process not an end in itself.

Yellow is for Sunlight; Sunlight as revelation. The clouds part and the sun is revealed! But without clouds there is no sun. Just as color is a concept discovered in ancient Greece, sunlight only exists as a defined element in its relationship to darkness. Sunlight is illumination both physical and metaphysical. But sunlight is not even light until objects and beings are lit by it. The objects and beings take on meaning only after the sun casts its light which is reflected on to the viewer as thought and feeling.

Green is for Nature. Life teems in the natural world, almost overwhelming the senses with its impact on everything from the majestic to the microscopic. It is a Turneresque vision of the world where nature is king and we are but followers, serfs and slaves. How human is nature. How natural is the human. Are we a part of it or just the observer. Like the discussion in Raphael's masterpiece 'The School of Athens", we live life in the space in between.

Turquoise is for Magic and Art. Turquoise is the space we inhabit between reality and the fantasy and needs to be filled with magic and art. The art is the process of transformation that happens when we set ourselves free to pursue the reality we choose, instead of the reality imposed on us each day when we wake. We are like the color turquoise that is suspended between green and blue. Between the churn of nature and the stillness of serenity.

Blue is for Serenity. The desire for serenity is not innate. Serenity in youth is often equated with death. "My, but don't the dead look peaceful and serene." It is only through growth and age that we accumulate angst, restlessness and discomfort and begin to realize that serenity in life is not death but contentment. Stillness in the storm of life is safety and sanctuary. Serenity between people is the ultimate thing to be desired. It is not easy or often but possible.

Purple for Spirit. There is a part of life beyond the known; the definable, the physical world of theories and proof. By admitting ourselves into our own spiritual realm we can, only then, find our true, purple selves. Without it, we are incomplete. Just a series of X's and Os. When we admit we are incomplete without the spiritual, we can begin the process of completing self-actualisation. The spirit is the part of ourselves we access to breach the walls of misunderstanding and enter into wordless consent. Spirits can rise and spirits can be broken. That's how we know we have them. But access to the spiritual realm is the key to life beyond tears and laughter.

CONTENTS

PINK: SEX

Status by Charlie Brodie

My heart thunders inside my chest.

I can feel the sweat sliding down my armpits, soaking the cream button up shirt that I had spent hours choosing. The hum of the restaurant floods my ears, a cacophony of voices that are fighting to be the loudest.

Joseph is staring at me.

'Are you okay?' He asks, worry looming over his words.

I nod my head, too afraid that my voice would break if I dared speak. His eyes drop from my face as he picks up his cutlery and begins to cut into his food. My stomach growls at me in response, but my mind refuses.

This is our fourth date. It had been the kind of meet cutes that you see on screen but think that it couldn't possibly be real or at least it would never happen to you. We had met at the beach. I had just finished swimming, seawater blinding me, when I mistook his blanket for mine and hadn't realised until a figure loomed over, eclipsing the sun.

We have spoken every day since, but a presence remains looming over me. A guilt shaped shadow blotting out the sun.

'Have I misread the situation? Are you not into me anymore?'

'No! No, you haven't misread anything.'

'Then what seems to be the problem? You're acting as if you're sitting across from your dead great aunt.'

A smile toys at the corner of his mouth and a nest of butterflies are unleashed in my stomach. I have to fight every single urge in my body to lean across the table and kiss him, but I am swiftly reminded why I chose this restaurant. A public setting to keep his reaction to a minimum. It doesn't take long for the butterflies to perish, leaving their shrivelled carcasses at the bottom of my stomach.

'I'm HIV positive,' I confess.

I stare down at my untouched pink salmon, focusing my eyes on it and wishing to shrink down to its size. The noise from the restaurant continues to surround me like a fog and I want to fold into myself, vanish like vapour.

I brace myself for impact, watching as he rests his cutlery onto his plate. His eyes dance around the restaurant, jumping from person to person until they settle on me. His face is unreadable and I begin to worry that the public setting won't subdue the anger I'm assuming is coming.

'Okay,' he says.

'Okay?' My eyebrows thread together like the closing of a wound.

He cocks his head to the side, searching for the words, and then nodding his head once he had found them.

'Well, are you managing it?'

For months I had sat with the news, an unwanted ghost that soured every morning, nights that would bleed together until every day felt like rising with wings of cement. The countless hours that I had sat on the floor of my shower, scrubbing until my skin was red raw, and the blood blisters that covered my shaking body.

I have not missed one doctor's appointment, have not forgotten to take one pill and my body is in the greatest shape that it has ever been in. I am the poster child for managing it.

'Yes, but you're okay with it?' I bring my head closer, afraid that our conversation will travel the restaurant like a bad smell. He leans in closer too, an understanding washing over his gentle face.

'Is your viral load undetectable?'

'Yes.'

'Then I don't see the issue,' he reasons. As he leans back in his chair, I am left with his words as they dance about my brain.

'I'm HIV positive,' I reply, believing that he hadn't heard me properly.

His hand reaches across the table and rests on top of my balled fist, softly stroking my white knuckles until they relax.

'I'm sorry.'

'What are you sorry for?' I ask, feeling like I should be the one to apologise.

'I'm not the first person you've been with since your diagnosis, am I?'

He was not. I had dated two men before him, men that I had met online and naively assumed there was a connection. One treated me as if I were riddled with a flesh-eating bacteria, brandishing me with names that burned into my skin. The other treated me as I were some new toy, a new experiment to leer at and fetishize, dehumanizing every atom of my being.

I shook my head, the memories leaving a sour taste in my mouth.

'I'm sorry that you've been made to feel ashamed. I am sorry that those men couldn't see you for the gentle, sweet human that you are.'

The outline of Joseph becomes less rigid as I struggle to keep the tears at bay, unable to stop a few breaking free. Joseph lifts his hand to my face, wiping the tear away as it fell. I close my eyes, allowing the restaurant to melt away.

'You've been really worrying about this, haven't you?'

I nod my head, thinking about the hours that I had spent tossing and turning last night, planning how I would break the news. Every scenario had ended with me sitting in the restaurant, alone, as Joseph flees.

His hand leaves my face and takes hold of my hand again, 'Christopher, this isn't something you should feel ashamed about.'

'I know,' I croak. 'I know, it's just hard because when people find out they no longer see me. All they see is this *disease*.'

'Christopher, you are not diseased. You're living with HIV, it's something you have. You're a lot more than your diagnosis, never let anyone diminish your worth, especially yourself.'

The waiter emerges by the side of our table, a smile plastered across her face.

'How's everything tonight?' She asks, eyes flitting from our faces down to our half-eaten meals.

'Perfect,' Joseph replies. 'Can we get our meals to-go and the check?'

'Of course!' She reaches down for our plates and heads back to the kitchen, ponytail swaying side to side like a pendulum.

'You want to go?' I ask.

Joseph's smile brightens his face as he chugs the last bit of his drink. He leans forward until our noses touch and I can feel the warmth of his breath as it fans my face.

'*We* are going to go,' he states. 'Can I kiss you now?'

I meet him the rest of the way, placing my lips against his. There is no fear crawling up my back at the thought of people staring, no worry that people would whisper. At this moment in time, sitting across from Joseph with our lips locked together, I could not care less about the world around me. Nothing else matters but this.

We break apart, but my lips carry the tingling sensation of Joseph's lips.

Joseph leans back into his seat, his arm resting over the side of the chair as he looks at me the way he looked at his meal. Hunger and desire, but not as if I were meat to be consumed. The kind of desire that is completely normal and not at all absurd for two grown gay men to have. Heat engulfs my body, my skin mirroring the untouched salmon that was once on my plate.

'Your place or mine?' He teases with a devilish smirk.

Pink To Make The Boys Wink by Daisy Woollerton and Teresa Woollerton

The first thing Flick heard when she woke up that Saturday morning was moans and groans coming from her bedroom floor. It took her some time to realise that she wasn't alone, her two aunts were staying with them and both sleeping on an airbed. By the sounds of the conversation, one of her aunts was about to be sick.

'Nooo, not there Sandra get up and do it in the loo!' That was Aunty Jenny, who probably didn't have as much to drink as Aunty Sandra, who was now clearly regretting it.

'I don't think I'll make it Jen'.

'Hurry up then, quick!'

Flick roused herself enough to say, 'don't let her be sick on my floor'.

When she was satisfied her bedroom floor remained vomit free, Flick fell back to sleep again.

The next thing that Flick noticed when she awoke, with the sun pouring through her bedroom window, was a bright frilly, bubble gum pink dress hanging on her wardrobe. The sort of pink that probably even supermodels couldn't get away with. The sort of pink that Flick, who wouldn't normally even wear a dress let alone anything quite so nauseating, was to wear today at her brother's wedding.

Her brother Mark was 10 years older than she was and had put his wedding off for a couple of years, partly due to the pandemic and because he and his fiancé Bronwen had been furloughed during that time. He had temporarily moved back into his old bedroom with his best man, Matt, for the night of the wedding.

Flick could hear her mum and her aunts in the kitchen putting the final touches to buttonholes for the wedding party. It seemed everyone was chipping in and helping at this wedding to save money.

'I can't believe she said that to you Debbie,' Sandra said. 'Not after all you've done.'

'Yeah, if she wanted a stately home, she should pay for one herself. Not bitch and moan about the Marquee in the pub gardens, that we've all bloody well put our hands in our pockets for. It's her bloody daughter getting married after all!' Jenny prided herself in saying just what she thought. Flick just wished she'd think a bit more before she said it.

'Well to be fair,' Debbie, flick's mum was always placatory, 'she just wanted a hotel for her only daughter. I can understand that, but all of us are feeling the pinch these days.'

'Oh, for God's sake,' Jenny retorted. 'Don't stand up for her Debbie. Bronwen doesn't mind, she's just happy to be getting married'.

Flick decided for once to skip breakfast and after taking a deep breath, put the bridesmaid dress on. Unfortunately, she still needed to go downstairs and ask for it to be fastened.

'Mum, can you do it up?' she asked.

'Oh Felicity, you do look lovely,' Aunty Sandra cooed.

Flick wrinkled her nose in disgust.

'How old are you now? Fourteen? Do you have a boyfriend yet?' Jenny enquired, bluntly.

'Of course not, do you love?' Her mum replied.

Flick decided there was no need for her to speak as the women around her would ask and answer questions for her. This was not a question she was comfortable with, as she didn't like any of the boys at her school. She did, however, have a crush on an older girl when she was a lot younger, but hadn't told anyone.

Aunt Sandra nudged her, 'Pink makes the boys wink'.

'Oh Sandra, stop it you're embarrassing her,' Jenny laughed.

Having been finally fastened at the back, Flick made her getaway.

'Make sure Mark and Matt are ready', her mum called after her. 'We're going in 30 minutes.'

Flick banged on Mark's door, Matt answered 'Oh god, what are you wearing?'

'Not my choice. Apparently "Pink makes the boys wink",' Flick told him.

'Or blink in total disbelief,' Mark replied.

'Anyway, mum says hurry up, we're leaving soon.' Flick was now very eager to get this day over with.

It was her brother's and Bronwen's day, but for her it was starting to become torture. Mark and Bronwen's circle of friends, as well as their money, had dwindled during the pandemic. So, her mum and aunts had invited distant relatives to help make up the numbers. She wasn't in the mood for drunk distant relatives questioning her, drunk close relatives were bad enough.

The wedding ceremony and breakfast, although a bit boring, went smoothly. However, the evening came and with it, copious amounts of alcohol, a DJ and her aunts' favourite, karaoke. Relatives Flick had never seen before sought her out and asked the inevitable. 'Your turn next Felicity', 'Who's the lucky fella?' or just 'well have you got a boyfriend yet?'.

One particular drunk, great uncle wouldn't leave it alone. 'So why haven't you got a boyfriend? A good-looking girl like you. What's wrong with you? You're not going through this lesbian phase that a lot of young girls go through now, are you? Wouldn't have happened in my day'.

Flick hastily made her escape and bumped straight into another wedding guest.

'Oh hi, sorry you must be Flick, I'm May.' Flick looked up, straight at a girl a bit older than her, and a lot better dressed in a smart top and jeans.

'I don't think I know you.' Flick suddenly felt self-conscious, which was amazing, partly because all the earlier intrusive questions had just made her irritable and now someone was speaking to her in a normal way. She felt tongue tied as though she should say something clever and funny, but just didn't know what.

'Oh,' May smiled 'I think our mums were friends at school'.

'I don't think I've met your mum'.

'Well,' May laughed 'She's on the stage singing 'Voulez Vous' with your mum.'

Flick turned and there they both were on the stage, doing their best impression of ABBA. Then Jenny and Sandra joined them, much to the delight of the other wedding guests clapping and cheering them on. Jenny, it seemed, did not learn her lesson from the night before and clearly thought that the 'hair of the dog' was a good hangover cure. There was a loud cheer as Jenny fell into the audience, landing on her back with her dress around her waist.

Flick was momentarily horrified, but Jenny soon got up and started dancing with the drunk great uncle from earlier.

'Oh God', May groaned, her eyes still twinkling with amusement. 'Let's go, it's only 10pm this lot have only just started, it will all just get a whole lot worse'.

'Where to?' Flick wanted nothing more than to spend time alone with this, cool older girl. Although she worried that she wouldn't know what to say or sound cool enough. Then there was the hideous dress, she was about to refuse her offer.

'Swings?' May suggested.

'Ok.'

They headed for the swings in the pub garden. A lot of the younger children had either gone home or were with their parents, so they were both alone.

'Love the dress Bo Peep,' May smiled.

'Oh, it's hideous, isn't it?' Flick groaned. She suddenly found her tongue, 'I didn't choose it. I think it was the victim of the money saving.'

May was laughing 'Oh my god, no wonder. Do you think they were sober when they chose it?'

Flick suddenly felt relaxed and happy in May's company, 'Who knows? I think they have some crazy idea that if they make me look feminine enough, I'll get a boyfriend. Apparently '"Pink, makes the boys wink" whatever that means.'

May just laughed, and then she turned, her bright eyes looking straight at Flick. 'And do you have one?'

Flick felt her pulse race and her mouth go dry. 'One what?'

'A boyfriend?'

'I've been asked that a lot today.' Flick looked down kicking the dirt with the toe of her shoe. 'But I don't… have a boyfriend that is.'

'Me neither, wish the aunties would stop asking.' May laughed.

Flick raised her head and met May's eyes. *I'm glad to hear it,* is what she wanted to say, but words failed her again. May's hair was shorter than Flick's and was slightly windswept by the cool breeze. Flick realised she was staring; her cheeks were probably as pink as her dress.

'Have you ever had one?' May asked her, after a slight hesitation.

'No… I've never really wanted one.'

'No girlfriend?'

This made Flick go from pink to red. Girls their age didn't have girlfriends, right?

'Sorry,' May's smile faltered slightly, 'I didn't mean to make you uncomfortable,'

Flick swallowed down her embarrassment. It was time to be bold.

'I, um, never met a girl I liked enough,' Flick kept eye contact with May, trying to keep steady on the swings.

Then loudly, from the pub Bronwen belted 'Heaven is a Place on Earth' into the microphone. She was a slightly better singer than the aunties, at least she was in tune.

May jumped off the swing and offered Flick her hand. 'Want to dance to shit karaoke?' she laughed.

Flick smiled as she took May's hand, pulling her body closer to hers.

The girls span each other around, stumbling and giggling in the garden lights.

Suddenly, the night wasn't so bad after all.

RED:
LIFE

Neuroqueer by Phoebe Webb

Neuroqueer: Being both neurodivergent and queer, with some degree of conscious awareness and/or active exploration around how these two aspects of one's being entwine and interact. – Dr. Nick Walker

It's said that your teenage years are when you discover who you truly are, to forge a sense of identity to carry into adulthood. This adage needs to get in the proverbial bin.

Those of us with a self-concept as lacking in depth as Boris Johnson is of integrity, panic that we are soulless husks, and the amorphous adolescent with complete conviction in who they are will see this projection crumble before their eyes when their prefrontal cortex reaches maturity a decade after the rest of the body.

The expectation to be a fully formed human being by our twenties is a recipe for existential crisis.

As pack animals, we are very reliant on external feedback and popular opinion to understand ourselves. Introspection is few people's strong suit; from birth we are conditioned to keep up appearances and forgo unfettered instincts. This could come with relative ease if you are aligned with the status quo, however any defiance has long justified alienation at best, or violence at worst.

Thus, as we (or others) become aware of idiosyncrasies that separate us from the pack, we are likely to opt for self-preservation in the form of repression and mimicry.

My poor understanding of societal customs, pathological people-pleasing, obsessive nature, and consequential lack of identity held hands in a circle and summoned mental illness. At least I had something for my personality to revolve around now. Paradoxically, considering mental illness impaired opportunities for true personal development, I became terrified of making healthy changes because it would rid me of all my substance as a person.

I saw peers go on to do what we're "supposed" to do, what *I* was supposed to do – or rather, become who I was supposed to *be*. They found their kin, went to university, discovered their passions and pursued lifelong career aspirations. Meanwhile I had nothing to do, nowhere to go, no one to be. Since my childhood imagination's projection of adulthood was evidently fantasy, I grasped onto the identity of "crazy" to not feel entirely void of substance.

This defence mechanism actualised my worst fear.

I began to question my sexuality in my early twenties. In hindsight this is very young, but at the time it seemed rather belated. An awkward and naïve social outcast, there was nothing during adolescence to evoke consideration that I was anything but heterosexual. I was 22 when I settled comfortably on calling myself bisexual, a revelation that coincided with a decision to fight my self-destructive neuroses in pursuit of recovery.

This meant stripping away the pseudo self-concept I'd crafted out of desperation in hesitant hope of discovering who else I could be. I can only describe this as terrifying and liberating (those words are more synonymous than we give them credit for). My newly discovered queerness contributed to the embryonic foundation of identity that facilitates recovery. With this came improved health, some semblance of social life, relationships, and becoming a cog in the capitalist machine. I ticked off some of those rites of passage I'd observed in my peers, years previous. Better late than never, I suppose. I'm doing what I'm supposed to.

But is it meant to feel this achingly performative? Like being dropped into a meticulously directed theatre production and being expected to instinctively know each sashay and soliloquy.

I'm an adult now, I should know who I am and what I'm doing. *Should*.

Surviving as a queer person requires performance. Bi- and pansexual folk are sometimes said to have "straight-passing privilege"; the suggestion that they can choose to live in a way that doesn't disclose their queerness, instead adopting a façade of heterosexuality to protect them from discrimination. Trans people are routinely told that if they don't want to be harassed, they should "stop pretending" and live as their assigned sex. People enter farcical marriages to have the implicitly demanded 2.5 children and white picket fence because coming out is not an option. This recital is to censor oneself, to repress natural inclinations, to camouflage any indicators of "other" in order to be what society tells us we *should* be.

At ages 27 and 30 respectively, I was diagnosed with ADHD and autism, which explained decades of feeling like an alien imposter. During those years I became progressively estranged from the concept of womanhood and started identifying as non-binary.

Neurodevelopmental differences and queerness may appear inconsequential, but many people find that those fundamental facets of self are unified by how they make navigating a cis/heteronormative, neurotypical world a labyrinth. Be it neurotype, gender or sexuality, they conjure feelings of otherness that are often hard to define: the simultaneous relief and dread felt when we discover there is vocabulary to describe our experiences; disclosing a fundamental part of ourselves over and over not knowing what the reception will be, or instead deciding to pantomime "normal" for fear of rejection. Ultimately, being unsure that you'll ever accept who you are.

It's with the starkness in these similarities that I declare I am not incidentally queer and neurodivergent: my queerness and my neurodivergence are entwined and inseparable.

Learning what it is to be neuroqueer is one reason I don't need to rehash maladaptive patterns to make a Frankenstein's monster of a sham identity. My brain's wiring was not made for prescriptive structures to tell me what I *should* be, so my attempt to conform created a chasm so vast that for years I was incapacitated.

The increased visibility of the LGBTQ+ and neurodivergent communities is unfortunately not met only with support and awareness, but also with publicised vitriol that denies our existence and dismisses our struggles.

In other words, the world is still not made for us. We are fully aware that suppressing our true selves could potentially protect us from those that don't value difference, but years of this practice is as big a threat to life. More and more of us are pulling earth-shattering power moves by opting to quit the performance and instead unveil our glorious ambiguity, knowing that with visibility comes epic fortitude.

Arachnida by M.K

In my body, I am seamstress
and designer and assassin
Deny yourself the fear of being me
Do you understand?

Your eyes refuse to leave me
Yet there is no admiration
Only revulsion at the groteseque
Must this body fit your formula?

My hunger is monstrous
I fear this gore will aid your agenda
Sickly consumption is my survival
So why are you watching me?

I beg for relief, white flag and all
But the hard wait is over
It begins as I feel barely contained
Are you seeing this?

The first tear, I'm travelling break neck

You see it slowly, little by little
Old habits wrenched from my body
Will this be over soon?

Silence stuns in the morning
Yesterday's guise already forgotten
Euphoria is my new colour
Don't I seem more palatable?

I will settle into this shell
And of course the hunger will return tenfold
But at last I will be received
Why won't you look at me now?

Darkness closes in on this freshly birthed flesh
The cycle starts again

Do you understand yet?

SONI by Ashley Hickson-Lovence
in loving memory of Justin. S. Fashanu

Just a Bernardo's-bred black boy, taken
Under the wing of Alf and Betty, who had
Swapped London for rural Norfolk and
Took in both, Justin, and his younger brother, John.
Interested in singing and boxing but when the canaries of
Norwich City came calling, football was the winner.
Scored a screamer against Liverpool in the cup,
Flicked the ball up and hit it sweet so unsurprisingly
A move to European Champions, Nottingham Forest, followed.
Signed for a million-pounds by Brian Clough in '81 but
His easy-going disposition off the pitch concerned some,
And with the bond with his brother breaking, there was
No-one to hug him, when he came out, and just eight years later,
Under some arches not far from where he was born, he hung.

ORANGE: HEALING

Walls With Windows by Rob Sadler

[Trapped in the impossibility of possibilities, which
elude tranquillity, I pretend].
There is no end.
Smiling through gritted teeth, my bleeding gums,
weeping,
Seep.
[We cannot reap, in un-sown sleep, the dog-eared
fragments of those we seek].
Oh, sunless sky, you lie!
You cheat!
*For far above the clouds, you wreak of late
expectations: behold the weak! ...*
*In blistered beams of hidden heat, we dare not speak
to those we seek.*
*Yet 'neath the gloom, your subjects, meek ... cower in
winter's outlook: bleak.*
Brighter days!
Shimmered haze, pulsate in tarmac's melting phase.
Potholes form, wrecking cars, reckless in their planet
scars.

['Veer not I tell you, steer your fear' – be forever far
away from here].
Avoiding paths long forgot, I mount the kerb,
curbing rot, the needy need us … tempting?
Knot.
To whom? I wander far beyond, where mindsets
meet the moribund.
In other words, I cannot muster the art of mining
souls which crushed her.
Take heed my friend, this time will pass.
Why gaze at shoes when there are stars?
In smother words, I cannot find the all-in front we
leave behind.
Looking back to what's ahead, scars which fade are
left unsaid.
[Above the neck up, knead that check-up: rewire this
able addled mind].

> *I.   Here.   You.   Now.   So long.*
> *Be.   Gone!*

I hear you now: place my arms around me in prism
light refraction beams.
Embrace uniqueness, even unrequited – turn your
inside out from quietus.
Why watch walls when windows welcome warmth?
For those of us of sensitivity, struggling with your
sense of pity,
I say this, unequivocally …
[*insert your hurt here*]. Live freely.

We are Valid by Lauren Bruen

For my whole life, I didn't know where I fit in. I felt different to my friends. I had an attraction for him, his hair, his eyes, and his charm. I had an attraction for her, her personality, her smile, and her laugh. I had an attraction for them, their confidence, their style, and their beauty.

How confusing…

My friends only had attraction for him.

My friends only had attraction for her,

Many had not considered or heard of them.

As a woman, we have so many obligations thrust upon us and our attraction or sexuality are no different. The world tries to convince young girls that women *should* only be attracted to men. Look at the movies, girls' toys, what we wear only to be sexualised by men, what society pushes on us, what the government pushes on us. This force pushing us to be girlfriends, wives, and mothers. No wonder we are confused and have little to no room to explore ourselves, our sexualities. As a woman, I was 'supposed' to only have an attraction for him.

Let's just ignore it, I told myself. Let's take those thoughts, feelings, and part of myself, and bury them all deep down.

I soon found out that it was not that easy to ignore.

My first sexual experience, kissing her, both trying to understand why we liked it. Confused and scared, thinking should we like it.

A romantic experience with a trans man, looking at them from across the room, staying up late chatting and flirting until 3am. Talking about a future together.

My long-term relationships with men, feeling the easiness of not feeling judged by society, and enjoying their masculinity.

They all felt the same to me. They all felt natural. They all felt fucking great.

But, what about the opinions of society, the patriarchal systems, and the government? They all claim I wasn't allowed to feel this way. We all need to fit inside the same box, that benefits these systems, and if we don't, we are outcasts. Outcasts of mainstream society, outcasts to our families, and outcasts to social circles.

From my teenage years to adulthood, my confusion only became more confusing. My longing for a place where I belonged became more passionate. My feelings of wanting to show the world me, the real me, only got more intense. I longed for a life where I wasn't an outcast, a place where queer people would feel accepted.

46

I was in a long-term relationship with the gender I was supposed to be with. So, I can't possibly talk openly now, right?

Wrong. There is never a time limit on you coming out or celebrating you.

I am pansexual.

I will not be silenced.

I will not be told who I can and cannot find attractive, have love towards and have romantic feelings or experiences with.

I will not be told that I cannot fancy a certain gender any less than another.

I turned to my community, the queer community. Finally, I fit in. But do I?

The sad truth of negativity breathes into all aspects of every community, and the queer community isn't any different. I felt judged and rejected by a community that was supposed to respect, love, and celebrate me. I felt on the outside, and I felt that I wasn't quite seen or heard. It hurt.

I wasn't queer enough.

I wasn't gay enough.

I 'can't possibly' have these same thoughts and feelings towards those of all genders.

But to the cis-gendered individuals,

I wasn't straight enough.

I 'can't possibly' have these same thoughts and feelings towards those of all genders and pronouns.

47

And for me, the answer is simple. I am who I am. I love who I love. I find attraction in who I find attraction to, regardless of gender.

I may be in the '+' but I am still just as valid.

So, please let's create a safe community for all queer people. For everyone that comes under our beautiful, (sometimes messy), but fucking fun and amazing LGBTQ+ rainbow umbrella. Let's celebrate our similarities as well as our differences.

The queer community offers so much goodness and I think we need to push that compassion, kindness, happiness, safety, and inclusive spaces so that all queer people feel welcome, supported, and valid.

Mind, Body, and Heart by Molly Gooding

Dearest past self,

You have turned seventeen and your future feels different. Walls have been constructed around you where endless pathways used to sprawl. Chasing after opportunity is no longer an option, running and leaving problems behind now an impossibility. Suddenly you are not able to walk like you once did and you are forced to slowdown, sit and think about secrets you have barely let yourself glance at. Truths that were whispered at the back of your head and quickly stamped on. Revelations that, if said out loud, some would not understand. Avoidance becomes second nature; the truth cannot hurt if not acknowledged.

Disability is not something you can avoid, in fact, it will hit you like a crashing wave, dragging you under whilst you cling to any relief like someone drowning clings to gasps of breath. It is not like all the other sicknesses you have had, there is no getting better from it. Healing feels out of reach, complicated and unachievable. But even though your life is on hold, the days, predictably, keep coming. Each day you learn something new about your body and you begin to listen. Pain becomes a familiar acquaintance, you'll probably never be friends, but you learn to cohabit.

The quiet rage and deep ache that occurs when cure-alls and miracles are suggested will slowly fade, an acceptance that those difficult suggestions are proof that people are good and are willing for you to feel less pain. A dawning understanding that human kindness is not perfect, leads to quiet conversations of shared knowledge and understanding. Advocation becomes second nature, a bravery you did not know you possessed will grow. The uncertain future will become less daunting, you know how to survive it now.

So, when thoughts you were avoiding catch up to you, questioning your identity and how to love, you greet them in the middle. Not as friend or foe, but simply as the truth. Reflecting on thoughts that were willed into silence is not easy to grapple with, and other people make it hard, but you know this route, you have travelled it before, even if the landscape has changed. Your understanding of your body and disability grants you the ability to understand your mind and heart.

That is how you begin to understand that healing is knowledge and learning.

Healing does not mean cured; it means empowered.

You will get there, I promise,
Your future.

YELLOW: SUNLIGHT

A Collection of Letters by R.W and M.K

Look alive! The sun is up and I'm thinking of you. It's been eight years of sunrises and I still remember the first one we shared. It was quiet. The back room of my parents house that I still call "my room" in the back of my mind. Do you remember how small it felt? That bed took up more than half the room, and it felt like an island in the world's smallest ocean. We didn't sleep, just sat there talking in the dark until it softened into light. We imagined braving the cold morning air and walking the half mile down to the beach to watch the sun rising over the most easterly point in Britain. I could have lived and died a thousand times in that bed with you. I learned how it feels to be loved by a person in that bed. Talking to you felt like - feels like - everything and more. Even now, with you far away, writing these words to be read by you feels like springs digging into my back and my brother brushing his teeth in the bathroom next door and Wes Anderson movies that we never get to the end of because we're love-drunk or tired or just not that into it. That bed in that room in that house was canvas and fortress rolled into one. The west-facing window would let in diluted sunlight, shining and stirring us from one dream to wake us into another. I think of you when the sun rises because it reminds me of waking up beside you. It reminds me of shirts worn inside out after the manic rush to the bus stop where I knew you'd be waiting with yellow light spackling the creases of your cheeks. I was always a morning person, but there's no feeling quite like waking up when somebody loves you.

R.W

I'm awake and the sun is no longer blue, but warm and golden. Not like those cold days after you left. Sleep barely left me; it stuck with me, as persistent as daylight. What are you doing right now? Getting ready for lectures? Sleeping in? Most of my time was spent wondering about you. Daydreaming. And fantasizing. And wanting. And missing you. The bus stop coming into view would fill my shoes with lead, movement felt impossible. We had so little time before you left. That sad, lonely shelter was missing something so vital. Someone. Life whipped around me like a storm, only thick, heavy. Those last few steps were like trying to wade through set honey. First my legs, then my whole body sank into the feeling. Drowning. Crushing pressure all around. Walls made of eyes getting closer and closer until I can practically feel them on my skin. Only the arrival of the bus would crack the cocoon I had wrapped myself in. Landing in the cheap leather seat it would hit me again; What are you doing right now? Are you okay? Do you miss me? That all-encompassing heaviness vanished with the ping of my phone. Reading your messages felt like being hit by a tidal wave, my anxiety peaking and dissolving all at once as they crashed over ignored emails and snoozed alarms. You weren't there in person to physically comfort me when the sight of my body sickened me. You didn't need to be, you made up for it with your words. You're the keeper of my most intimate thoughts, I've never had a second thought about honesty. Our ideals always were intertwined. Any ounce of fear dissipated briskly whenever I pressed send. You were my refuge and safety. The lonely bus journeys I had invented for myself were a facade. They were in fact filled with your music and your words and thoughts of you. An abundance of love. Sunlight felt warmer filtered through those grimy bus windows. What are you doing right now?

M.K

Things got easier around the middle part, didn't they? Our love had reached its highest point. I had hoped so badly that when I left my parent's house and my room behind it would be with you, to start the life we talked through our phone screens about for all of those lonely years. Now you are closer to me than I ever knew you

59

could be. You share my bed and my kitchen and the space in front of my T.V so often that if I close my eyes and think hard enough I can convince myself that dreamed-of life has begun. I had to get a job. Then another. Then another. I felt your arms wrap tight around me every time I got the offer. I heard your voice and the support couched within it every time I came home shaking with the urge to quit. Sometimes I time myself walking home from the latest job, desperate to count out the minutes that belong to me and those that I sell for minimum wage. I shaved minutes off my record one night, when I knew you were waiting for me. I saw the light on in the window as I turned onto the street, blessed myself for getting that second key cut and started hammering the rain-slick pavement in half-wrecked work shoes already hammered by the daily commute. That little square of warm, you-filled yellow lit up the black street, like a portrait of the midday sun out of place in the world's saddest art gallery. My hand found my keys in my pocket and gripped so tight the teeth might have bitten my palms if I hadn't made it to the door so quickly. I clawed my way in because my life did depend on it. I've told you so many times that I'm barely a man, not in any way that matters. When I arrived panting and dry lipped from the wind that tried to keep me from you I knew that was true. Whatever I was, whatever I am when I'm with you, it exists outside of jobs, gender, money, or art. It exists solely for the love of you.

R.W

The sun peeking softly through drizzling clouds, we strolled out of York rail station trying to make sense of our directions. A weekend getaway had felt medicinal. It was the opportunity to exist as our authentic selves in a place far from the lives we left behind. This city did not know us. Anxiety receded at the feeling of your hand in mine while we walked historic streets in search of a drink. The expensive whiskey we drank at the Cat in the Wall turned out to be secondary to the mindless conversation. I could talk forever with you about nothing in particular. One overarching topic we would edge often was the idea of a home. Our home. York was a reinforcement that we could make anywhere our home, that as long as I'm with you I feel safe. My worries are heard, my bad thoughts comforted. There was no point on our trip away that I had any longing to go back to Suffolk. Even as I stood in the queer art exhibition, overwhelmed with tears at the sight of Saint Agatha looking towards Heaven in ecstasy as she held her severed chest. Raw feelings of dysphoria and euphoria enveloped my body. In that moment I had wanted to run and hide from the feeling, and it was your arms that guided me to facing it. Your adoration felt sempiternal; I could exist in another shell and you would love me just as much. I think you sometimes forget the words you say to me, but I do not. As we sat in our hotel, making a mess on the pristine bed sheets with our Chinese takeaway, your words wrapped around me like a warm blanket. The home we build together will be reminiscent of that night; shared secrets, frivolous ideas, indulgences, desires, and comfort.

M.K

I used to think I knew what love was before you. It was a high school crush on the sickly looking skater boy and his androgynous friend whose gender wouldn't matter even if I could remember it. It stayed a crush until it went away, which I hoped against hope every day that it would. I thought love was when you liked somebody so much it physically hurt. I dreamed of suffering enough that the love would leave me alone. Love and pain may well have been the same thing as far as I was concerned. Not to be talked about and not to be acted on if you valued your manhood. You changed that when you taught me that the parts that make up a person matter less than the whole. Love is transcendence. It's a place to simply be. That is exactly what you are to me and I solemnly promise that I will spend the rest of my days trying to be that for you. I'll live with you, marry you, cook a thousand meals with you and grow old by your side in the place that we make together. Eventually the sun must set, of course. All good things come to an end, sure, but what about better things? Do we have eyes on the afterlife? Do we know beyond a shadow of a doubt where love goes? All the heady days I'll spend with you, where we'll breathe one another in like fresh air and I'll feel your hands on my skin like gentle rays of sunlight - they have to go somewhere. Wherever they go I hope we follow. I hope there are bus stops and warm yellow windows and Japanese whiskey and beds too big for the rooms that try to contain them. I hope Saint Agatha looks up at us and smiles.

R.W

Constellations by Ellen Freeman

Sunlight dapples her skin,
golden hues among the freckles
I have turned into constellations
with my fingers,
more times than I can count.
She comes to life under the sun's
rays, eyes alight, face turned
like the most beautiful of
sunflowers.
I wonder what I would have to do
to have her turn to me like that;
seeking, loving, awestruck.
Her fingers twine with mine,
paint-covered. I trace the lines
nature engraved into her ochre skin,
her heart-line, life-line, fate line.
My fingers trace her skin, and I wonder,
not for the first time, if her fate
is entwined with mine.

GREEN: NATURE

Under Starry Skies of Rust by Rob Sadler

March across the greening fields now nubile shoots of sage. Wetted winds of lighter days lick skin with sun-kissed haze, budding branches bring bursting blossoms awake from dormant slumber. Buzzards soar on thermals high above the thawing tundra.

April brings the buxom bittern afraid in shadowed reeds, nestled in the shallowed nooks of salty sea-breached fields. Cuckold cuckoos cock their heads in newly nestled nests. Birdsong fills the chorused dawn as swallows swoop on heat.

May blossoms fall upon the ever-fragrant clover, the darling buds and bedded plants are bursting out all over. Yielded fields of tallish wheat greet the sunning amber, foot fell paths of hardened mud await the avid rambler.

June brides in garish garb marry one another. Morning suited booted men exchanging vows together. Bouquets flung in summer air await the baying throng, the longest day for making hay is whilst the sun shines on.

July the sky so wide and dry from eventide to dusk, sit with friends in Ipswich parks under starry skies of rust. Hammerhead clouds rise for miles above the stormy vista, thunder speaks with rain unleashed in sheets upon the river.

August bakes the madding crowds in coastal towns and beaches. Making hay the harvests lay their stacks of bales and wheat sheafs. Apples drop oh so close from the tree they fell from, drunken wasps seek sweeter flesh - much swatting in the maelstrom.

September cools a climate changed yet summer fires still smoulder. The leaves of youth begin to fall as nature starts to slumber. Whilst rains return and rivers run again to rising seas, the last Pride marches raise their flag to colourise the breeze.

October wisps in greying air as shorter days encroach, the heat begins to dissipate as longer nights approach. In coming out full be of hope, this life is ours to saviour, be at one with who you are and live forever green with nature.

The Morgen by Will Davidson

Tread the wooden boards
That loop around the Lound Lakes,
Moss ridden and brittle from time and damp,
And let the wind-lilting leaves brush your shins as
they sing.

The water is calm here,
No signs of the life below the lilypads
Or the thin sheen of surface scum.
From your place behind the treeline the world at
last is still.

Memories of a childhood,
Summer afternoons on a leaky boat.
An old man and a child bearing fishing rods,
Sat in wait, unsure what lies beneath the surface.

It could have been this lake.
Or any other, really.
The place matters less than the feeling it brings.
Home was in the darkest corners. Sight unseen.

Little fox girl, they called you when you traipsed
in after dark.
Hackles raised at the word. Cheeks redder than
the scrapes on your knees.
Never knew which part bothered you.
Little? Or girl?

Of course you know now.
The change in you stares back from the stillness
of the lake.
It takes a shape all of its own.
A morgen, a marid, a merrow.

'Who you were is gone now,'
The nymph appears to say.
It's breastless chest rising so softly
The water hardly stirs.

'Allow yourself some space at last,
Smell the ocean air blowing in from the east.
Watch the early sunrise and spread your wings
With the gulls and the kittiwakes.'

'Startle yourself with every word that you speak,
with a voice that has never been more *yours*.
Relearn the outlines and the boundaries of
yourself,
As teacher, student, and child of the woods.'

The words ring true, you've spent too long

Holding onto a you that shouldn't have been.
Trace the Merrow's brilliant path.
And see the new world that awaits in the wake of your reflection.

TURQUOISE:
MAGIC & ART

Love and Honey Bread by Ellen Freeman

I watch as she turns, face half illuminated in the moonlight. Goosebumps shiver over my skin, a deep chill in my bones that I'm not sure came from the sea air. I'm starting to think it's from being close to her. The sea drags itself up the beach, mumbling as it washes her footprints from the sand.

Grace collapses beside me, hair falling across her face. 'Have you been waiting long?'

'I have no idea.' I sigh, rubbing my hands. They're numb, and slowly turning a shade of purple that would be pretty if it wasn't painful.

Grace takes my hands in hers, blowing on them gently. 'You should be wearing gloves.'

'And you should have been here an hour ago.' I counter, eyebrows raised.

Grace groans, tucking our hands under her scarf. 'I know, I'm sorry. You know how I get on-'

'On Beltane. Yes, I do know.' I agree. Grace's brain works at a hundred miles an hour, her mind always whirling. At Beltane though, her mind is nothing short of a whirlwind. She's always coming up with new ways to celebrate, new alter decorations, or rituals planned.

'You should see my mum's altar. It's even more elaborate than last year's!' Grace grins, eyes wide with wonder and excitement. 'Did you decorate your altar?'

'I used the flowers you gave me.' I tell her, because I know that's what she wants to hear. Sure enough, her smile widens.

'Did you do any baking?' she asks, letting my hands go so that I can retrieve the bread she knows damn well I've baked. I break a piece off and hand it to her. She eats it quietly, staring out at the sea as she chews. 'I like the honey, it's very sweet.'

When I don't say anything, Grace leans her head on my shoulder and points into the distance. 'I just saw a mermaid, did you see her?'

'It's too murky in Dunwich for a mermaid.' I grin, unable to keep from laughing.

'A Selkie then!' Grace grins, grabbing my hand again and squinting into the darkness.

'We don't have seals here either.' I remind her.

'Actually, they have been spotted,' she tells me, chin held high. When she sees my raised eyebrow she sighs, rolling her eyes. 'Fine, *once*. One was spotted *once*.'

'Maybe they've come because they know we'll believe.' I smile, combing her hair with my fingers as she rests her head back on my shoulder. Grace always smells of incense and some earthy perfume I'm sure she made herself.

'You smell of honey bread.' she tells me, as if she's read my mind. I break another piece off and pass it to her, chewing absentmindedly on my own piece. The moon is dipping lower, its light reflecting on the sea as it ripples below us. It's these moments with Grace that I've learned to treasure. The companionable silences where just being beside her soothes my nerves.

Something glitters in the sand and stones below us, sparkling like a star that has fallen from the sky. Grace spots it at the same moment, jumping from our perch and rushing to retrieve it. I watch her move, all curves and elegance. My graceful Grace. She picks the treasure up, inspecting it in the starlight.

'Well, what have you found?' I call, because she's got that look on her face that means she's dreaming up a new story. That's the thing with Grace: everything has a story.

Hopping up beside me again she extends her hand, showing me the perfect golden chain. It's so dark I can barely make out the pendant that hangs from it, nestled in the arch of Grace's thumb. The stone is somewhere between blue and green.

'It's turquoise,' Grace confirms, holding it up under the streetlamp that's flickering above us half-heartedly.

'We should hand it in to the pub.' I tell her, nodding in its direction. Grace pulls a face.

'Why? I found it,' she shrugs.

'Someone's lost it, Gee.' I nudge her. 'And it looks expensive.'

'Who says someone's lost it?' she frowns, rubbing her thumb over the stones. 'Who says it wasn't here for us to find? Maybe it's pirate treasure, or the discarded gift of the heartbroken human lover of the most beautiful mermaid to have ever lived!'

I'm about to argue, but I see that twinkle in her eye, and I decide to play along. 'Or, maybe the Selkie left it for us.' I grin, looking back out at the rolling waves.

'Somebody wanted us to have it.' she agrees, still inspecting the pendant like she's never seen it before. Like she didn't hide it there hours ago. Like she hasn't been waiting for me to spot it. Like I said, Grace loves a story.

'Here,' she says, brushing my hair over my shoulder. She clasps the necklace and leans back, admiring it where it lays over my heart. She kisses me, her hand warm on my cheek. I've been outside so long I'm surprised I can feel it. The streetlamp flickers out entirely, leaving us stranded beneath the moon and stars.

'Do you think she sees us?' Grace whispers, her breath warm against my skin.

'Who? The Selkie?'

'No,' she laughs. 'The moon.'

I pull my jacket round us both as Grace starts shivering, the cold finally creeping in. 'Yes, I suppose so.'

'Beltane is my favourite time of the year.'

'Because I make honey bread?' I tease, watching her from the corner of my eye.

'No, because we met on Beltane!' she shoves me, but she's grinning.

I gasp, grabbing her arm in mock confusion. 'Wait, we did?'

'You're the worst!' she shoves me again, before pulling me into her arms. The wind runs its fingers through our hair, and we sit quietly in the starlight, listening to the waves mumble below us. The street is still, the air cool and fresh against our blushing skin.

'It's my favourite too.' I confess, twining my fingers through hers.

Between These Two Rocks by Charlie Brodie
Responding to Henry Scott Tuke's 'The Critics'
(1927)

between these two rocks
with sand nestled between our toes
there is safe harbour here
a place we can call ours

your body, beautiful and bare
the sun kissing places my lips crave
i am adrift at sea
lost to this tempest I name love

our eyes meet from across sea to land
your lips forming words that are lost to my ears
i submerge myself under water
wishing you would follow

as I remerge, he is whispering into your ear
honey dripped from a serpents tongue
the tide holds me back, secure in its grasp
my body longing to be dry

the sun falls from the sky
a ball of flame melting into the horizon
casting this beach into darkness
the shadows swallowing our heat

i call to you but you do not hear
a roar that turns into a whisper
siren to a sailor
shipwrecked on the jagged edges of your body

we are standing alone in the shallows
our bodies curling around one another
whispering secrets
as the last ray of sun disappears

the seabed cuts at my feet as I search for you
in the crevices of your body
our harbour lost to the falling sun
time pushing us back to land
    we will always have daylight, between these two
    rocks.

INDIGO:
SERENITY

My Bisexual Journey with *Heartstopper* by Francesca Mulvey

For as long as I can remember, I have always loved reading. The first book I ever received was *The Complete Illustrated Stories of Hans Christian Andersen* from my dad. At bedtime as a child, he would often read the tales to me in hopes of lulling me to sleep. The is the reason I love reading so much today - books on and inspired by myths and legends, and fantasy books mostly, though I enjoy other genres too, including graphic novels.

In short, books and storytelling have always been an integral part of my life. Dad would often make up his own stories to entertain me and my sister when we were younger, during our stays at Simonshof, a holiday home and farm in The Black Forest in Germany during the summer holidays. Each night me and my sister would get into bed, the sounds of crickets and the farm animals as they bedded down themselves for the night drifting in through the window, as Dad began yet another of the tales of adventure, that he would make up each year for our enjoyment, about Prince Poo-Poo who would fart to get himself everywhere – very entertaining for two children of around 4 and 5 when the tales began.

I am also autistic. This, as well as my overwhelming love for books, is as much a part of myself and my identity, and has been from the moment I was born. Even before my diagnosis at nineteen, I had always known. Always had a feeling, that I was "different" to other children. I had trouble grasping even the basic of social cues when it came to social interaction and struggled to maintain friendships the way I do now. I found myself mentally exhausted almost every day, and didn't know why, compared to my peers who didn't seem to have trouble with their energy levels. I was often a target for bullying, both because of my weight, and because I was easy to manipulate into believing things that weren't true, due to my yet undiagnosed condition. Despite this fact, I had friends, including my best friend who I have known since I was 5.

My love for books, and my autism, have always been two points of certainty in my life. My sexuality, however, is something I was not entirely certain of until around April of last year, after the *Heartstopper* Netflix adaptation was released. This wasn't the first time I had encountered the sensation that was *Heartstopper*, a graphic novel series where two boys are sat together, gradually become friends, and fall in love. Back in 2019 I was wandering around town in Ipswich where I live, and spontaneously decided to pop into Waterstones to see if they had any new books that I might be interested in.

I had barely stepped through the door and turned into my usual haunt - the Middle Grade/ YA section - when I spotted the colourful cover and title of a graphic novel, called *Heartstopper: Volume 1*. Intrigued by the cover, I picked it up and read the blurb: "Boy meets boy. Boys become friends. Boys fall in love," looked up at me between two pairs of shoes facing each other. I had a quick flick through and became instantly hooked by the art style and the characters themselves, and the unfolding story between central characters Nick and Charlie. I very quickly fell in love with *Heartstopper: Volume 1* and its characters (bar a few unpleasant ones) and couldn't wait to buy the next one when it came out.

I devoured the next instalment in less than a day and, as the series progressed, I began to realise how much I related to Nick in certain ways - but couldn't figure out why. Flash forward to 22nd April 2022, the day of the Netflix series adaptation release. After work I set myself up with a Margarita pizza, and garlic pizza bread, from Domino's and a load of treats, binge-watching the whole series that night.

As expected, I loved it as much as I had the graphic novels - and now, seeing at least a part of the graphic novels played out on the screen, I found Nick even more relatable than I had when reading the graphic novels, but still couldn't put my finger on why. I re-watched the series three times after the first and on the third rewatch, during a particular episode, I just started crying. I'd gradually realised, over the course of watching and then rewatching the series, and also rereading the graphic novels alongside this, the reason why I'd always related to Nick more than other characters.

I was bisexual. Though for me it was the other way round, having predominately always liked boys. I'd wondered for a long time whether I might be, since maybe Year 9 of high school, but I'd never felt overly certain of the possibility, and hadn't known anyone back then in 2010, who was openly bisexual and so had nobody my own age to confide in. The relief at finally feeling fully true to myself had me in floods of tears. It was like the final piece of a puzzle within me had slide into place. New possibilities that hadn't been there before, seemed to open up before me once I realised that final part of myself.

Thanks to Alice Oseman and her amazing series, I knew.

I was bisexual. I was finally, fully, myself.

VIOLET: SPIRIT

Mirror by Hex Cooper

I don't see myself in the mirror.

That's about the only way I can put it. I see the body that has grown and aged around me. The smudgy eyeliner makes me look frightening. The black clothes that wrap around the muscle growth I've worked so hard for. I see legs and feet, arms and a torso, a head, and everything else.

I see me. But it's not me, not really.

This isn't to say that I dislike every part of my body. I find joy in literally picking out the areas of neutral ground, tapping them with my fingers as I mentally count them. The slight curve of muscle that fans from my arms to my broad shoulders. My long legs, bony fingers, oversized rib cage; and the slight peak of my collarbone hidden away under my braids, a hairstyle that thrives on neutrality and provides a safe and scratchy curtain for me to hide in when the world is too much. I have parts that I like. Parts that I'm proud of. Parts that don't bother me at all.

But it's still not my body. Because it's not neutral like me. It's never me.

It doesn't belong to me.

The weight of a secret that people force you to keep can be so draining to carry. I have to wonder if the me inside is actually standing at this point, or if they've sagged under the weight and suffocation of being hidden away like I have time and time again. If their voice is hoarse from screaming into a pillow, their eyes sore from wiping tears, and their knuckles bloody and swollen from the frustration of it all because for fucks sake, why? Why, why why why?

Why does my mother hate me? Why does my brother disregard me? Why do my colleagues whisper about me, misgender me, and deadname me? Why do I have to live with "Oh, but I love your old name" and "You used to be so pretty" while being subjected to people pleading for body parts that make me nauseous at the sight of them as they cry "you're taking the child I love away from me"!

It's always what everyone else wants. What everyone else needs. It's always way too hard or sounds too off. Too confusing, too unimportant, too new to be real, sounding just like someone attention seeking because they want to feel important and special.

When does this body get to be mine?

When does the real me stop feeling like a tethered balloon? Like a ghost floating just out of reach?

It's too much for them. I'm too much for them.

And because of that, it will never be enough for me.

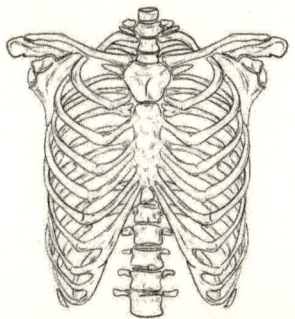

Oceans Apart or Magkahiwalay ang mga karagatan by James Williams

Memories are like water.

They can be fickle and melt away as snow does with the warmth of spring, or they can trigger a tsunami that leaves nothing but wreckage and trauma. Those moments we experience ripple out and have the potential to flood across the rest of our lives whether that be from a child tossing a pebble, or a mother duck gliding a path for her ducklings to follow.

Even before I sat there by The Round Pond with Christchurch Mansion watching over my shoulder, I knew whatever was about to happen was going to be one of the most turbulent moments that I'd ever experience in my life.

I could only hope the dark clouds I saw reflected in the water were just mother nature mocking the dark circles beneath my eyes.

I had turned every possible scenario over in my head, trying to weigh up which one would be the most likely so I could prepare myself and not be drawn into

111

the false hope my friends had tried to stifle my anxiety with.

But your mum is so sweet, she'd never do that.

Why would she ruin anything when you're her only son? She loves you.

But I thought you said your mum had family friends who were gay? That wouldn't make sense.

But unlike my friends, I knew that the only outcome of coming out to my mother was going to be a negative one. What I didn't expect was the silence that stretched between us like an ocean dividing continents. If it wasn't for the quacking of ducks and the gleeful screams of kids in the distance, I wouldn't have believed time was still moving with how my body had all but turned to stone.

My lungs burned, begging for breath, but it felt as if any movement, no matter how small, would shatter this moment around me and let in the torrent of my mother's rage that was rushing in to consume me.

But when it came, she did not shout.

No crashing waves at the shore.

Just a quiet flood.

Steady, yet powerful.

Destructive beneath the surface. Violence hidden in her words.

'There is no *gay* in the family,' she scoffed.

I blinked in shock. Even knowing it was coming, my heartbeat stuttered with my panic. I turned to see her staring straight ahead and I noticed her usual warm brown eyes had darkened. I couldn't remember the last time I felt fear, looking at my mother like that.

The all-consuming anger I could sense simmering below that calm façade was enough to give me goosebumps.

'Well, there is now.' I said quietly, but firmly.

I didn't even know why I said it. My mouth formed the words before I realised what I was saying. The look my mother snapped towards me of pure rage and loathing was enough for me to flinch. Then I was frozen again, caught in a stand-off with my mother.

An eternity stretched between us.

Two souls on either side of a river.

The roar of its turbulent waters heard in the heartbeat pounding in my ears.

Whilst my eyes were transfixed in those pools of burning mahogany, past the tears unwillingly starting to blur my vision, I could see the warped silhouette of Christchurch Mansion over my mother's shoulder. In that glimpse, my mind was led away from that moment to the thought of how much Christchurch Mansion and its grounds had seen of my life. How it had borne witness to my childhood and my teen years when I came to the park with my parents and friends. How it had also provided a place of refuge to my freshly migrated mother coping with the loneliness as a young Filipina stranded oceans away from her home and her family.

Now, it again bore witness to my family's suffering.

My mother stranded a second time from her family, only this time from the son she had birthed and raised. A chasm of her own creation. Though instead of oceans drawing us apart, it was ignorance and bigotry that cleaved a river between us, its banks crumbling away, flooding to become a lake, a sea, seemingly shoreless and uncrossable.

The manor continued to watch eternity unfold before it, in this stare down between mother and son, and it led me to wonder just how different this moment could have been.

Somehow, somewhere, maybe there was a reality where this woman embraced her son with nothing but love and acceptance. Maybe one where this conversation was avoided altogether and it was just another regular catch up in a park. One where this woman could welcome adopted grandchildren in open arms rather than cower at them like changelings from foreign wombs. One where this woman had never migrated to the UK and had a son to disapprove of. One where this woman's homeland had never been colonised and who you were or loved was never something challenged until those from foreign shores came and wreaked violent change upon us. In that reality we would not be sat here by this duck pond.

Who we were would not be the by-product of Western violence.

We would not be here at all.

But we are.

We are sat here. In this park, facing one another.

Caught up unwittingly in the ripples of violence and intolerance history has dealt us.

'Don't tell anyone about this,' she says calmly. 'Especially anyone in the family, alright.'

Eternity shattered around us.

A tidal wave crashing into me with more destructive force I thought feasible.

She turned back to face The Round Pond, posing more an instruction than question.

I hummed in agreement, knowing if I spoke properly my voice would break the same way my heart already had.

'We don't want them finding out.'

'I wasn't going to tell them anyway,' I add quietly.

'You shouldn't tell anyone.'

I scoffed before I had a chance to stop myself. My throat tightened as she glared at me once again, and I wondered just how many waves this tsunami would tear across my shore.

'I'm serious.'

Before I could relax my throat enough to respond, she had already gotten up from the bench.

'Don't be late home, we have dinner soon. It'll go cold otherwise.'

And then she walked away. A tide retreating as calmly as it had arrived. I was a child left adrift in the ruins of her devastation, and I could only wonder *What happens now?*

*

Once I was sure she had left, the dam I used to hold back the flood building behind my eyes broke free and the first tear sluiced down my cheek. I had to shut my eyes against the streams that started pouring as I let the waves of emotion crash into me and rock my shoulders with the force as I drowned.

It wasn't until the tide retreated, quenched from my despair, that I started to feel something light tickling the back of my hand. It persisted the longer I sat there. I opened my eyes and the light pattering I felt on my hand stopped.

A white winged butterfly had perched on the top of my hand.

For a few moments it sat there, slowly opening and closing its wings, before it fluttered up onto my chest, its head angled up towards me. It reminded me of a time when I was growing up where my mother told me about Filipino superstitions, and one in particular where it's believed that butterflies are the spirits of a deceased loved one coming to pay a visit.

Looking down at the butterfly perched on my chest, I wondered which of our family it was that had come to show me the love my own mother couldn't.

Notes on the writers or their stories

Charlie Brodie

Charlie Brodie is a writer based in Norfolk but has predominately studied in Suffolk. They have previously worked as a Co-Editor for the LGBT segment of Student Life and spends most of their time writing stories that are focused on queer youth and life. Charlie attained their bachelor's degree in English at the University of Suffolk in 2020. They successfully completed their studies on the MA Creative and Critical Writing at University of Suffolk in 2023 and is currently working on their PhD proposal. They are currently writing a novel that is a queer adaptation of Shakespeare's Romeo and Juliet. Charlie is partnering with The Hold in Ipswich to curate and showcase an art and literature exhibition that highlights Suffolk Queer Voices through the theme of Metamorphosis. They are also the main editor for *Suffolk Pride: We are the One in Five*.

Daisy Woollerton

Daisy is a writer, a MA student and she has been published in the University of Suffolk's 2023 anthology, *Suffolk Reflections*. She wanted to be involved with this anthology as she wanted to write something that reflected the early days of self-discovery, when becoming aware with one's identity and sexuality. Luckily her mother had a great idea for a story which they both incorporated with the colour pink, which becomes a symbol of femininity within the story. She loves cats, horror stories and a good rom com.

Teresa Woollerton

Teresa works for the NHS, writes a bit and loves a good party. She has co-written with her daughter, Daisy, to write the short story *Pink to Make the Boys Wink*. She says, '*I didn't think of being involved in the anthology initially, but then on a long car journey home the story just came into my head from start to finish. Daisy added her magic and there it was.*'

Phoebe Webb

Phoebe Webb is a neuroqueer trainee therapist, lived experience practitioner in the treatment of children and adolescents with eating disorders, and campaigner for all things relating to neurodivergence and mental illness. In her twenties, both her queerness and neurodivergence emerged into their consciousness like a jack-in-a-box, simultaneously a huge surprise and not remotely shocking. These facets of her identity have an indelible influence on how she practices counselling, peer support, and campaigning on and offline. Everyone experiences life intersectionally and she endeavours to influence change to make mental health provision as accessible and effective as possible, always with a combination of lived experience and elevating the voices of others. They describe themselves as an "occasional writer" with tenfold more ideas than finished pieces, and enjoys using essay and article formats to ponder over observations of the human experience or to channel self-righteous anger directed at the world into something productive!

M.K

Arachnida was written for all of the trans people facing scrutiny and abuse every single day. And all whilst dealing with their own gruelling dysphoria. Our transformations don't have to look pretty to other people, and they don't have to happen all at once. Making any kind of small change to feel better in your body should be a celebration. We deserve euphoria.

Dr Ashley Hickson-Lovence

Dr Ashley Hickson-Lovence is a novelist and part-time university lecturer with a PhD in Creative and Critical Writing from the University of East Anglia.

He is the author of two novels, *The 392* and *Your Show,* with his third book, *Wild East,* to be released with Penguin in May 2024.

Lauren Bruen

Lauren is a committed activist that has worked with many young people within the queer community, providing them with safe spaces to share their stories and life experiences. She has also previously volunteered for Suffolk Pride. She works as a Project Manager for a charitable organisation, working to help people feel more connected to their communities. Lauren believes that the power of voice is important, which is why she was inspired to write a piece for *Suffolk Pride: We are the One in Five.*
She also came out in 2022 and saw this as an empowering opportunity for herself, those who have already come out, allies and those who will come out in the future.

Rob Sadler

Rob is an Ipswich born writer who graduated with a first honours degree in English from the university of Suffolk. He writes poetry commissions for subjects ranging from mental health awareness to armistice day commemorations. In 2022 Rob was shortlisted for the Suffolk New Angle Prize competition with his story Salt Cellars, which can be found in the book Suffolk Arboretum. He is about to commence studying for a Masters in English Literature: Critical & Creative Writing. Rob enjoys acting, singing and public speaking - plus the renewed excellence of his beloved ITFC.

Molly Gooding

Molly Gooding is a creative that is based in Suffolk that explores their experience with identity and disability in their work. She is currently studying Childhood: Disability at the University of Suffolk, which helps to influence their creative work.

R.W and M.K

R.W and M.K are a Suffolk born queer couple, though are not out to everyone in their lives right now. They don't want their anonymity to take away from the pride they feel being queer. Written in the form of love letters to shape an incomplete picture of a bond looked back on. This piece was written to illustrate the hardships of long distance relationships, to have the only person who knows you as you truly are somewhere far away. It was also written to express that however hard things get, love is unwavering - love is the point of it all.

Ellen Freeman

Ellen Freeman is an author and poet from Suffolk. She is a Writer in Residence at the Van Gogh Museum

Amsterdam and is currently working on a collection of essays and poetry inspired by the artist's life. Ellen was shortlisted for the Canterbury Festival Fiction Prize in 2022 and longlisted for the New Angle Fiction Prize in 2023. Ellen is currently studying MA Creative and Critical Writing at the University of Suffolk. She graduated from the Open University's BA English Literature and Creative Writing programme in 2021. Ellen is the author of two muddle grade fantasy novels and is currently working on a Greek Mythology retelling. In her spare time, Ellen runs book-related social media pages, and buys more books than she could every possibly read.

Will Davidson

Will Davidson is a poet and writer based in Lowestoft. His work explores the beauty to be found in the horrific and mundane while maintaining a leftist voice, finding inspiration in authors such as Alison Rumfitt (Tell Me I'm Worthless) and China Mieville (The City and the City). There is a close connection to be found between Will's writing and his surroundings - to live and work in a place seemingly forgotten by time summons the loneliness and desperation in his words, banished only by the sense of community that can be found at the edges of small-town society. Queer experience is too often made out to be an endless tale of misery, and that is something Will challenges in his poem "The Morgen".

Francesca Mulvey

Francesca 'Fran' Mulvey is an autistic writer based in Suffolk, where she has lived since the age of five. She studied for a BA in English, and an MA in Creative and Critical Writing at the University of Suffolk, where she subsequently worked as a Student Experience Ambassador and a Student Life Adviser. Fran recently finished writing an own voices, middle grade fantasy inspired by the myth of the Greek goddess Hestia, which she is currently editing and plans to send to agents in the near future. When not writing fantasy fiction, Fran spends most of her time reading, watching a lot of KDramas and listening to KPop (mostly Stray Kids), studying Korean, and painting when the inspiration hits.

Hex Cooper

"To the child that cried themselves to sleep for years because two people told you to be silent. Fuck them. Those that would lock a bird in a cage don't deserve the privilege of hearing it sing.

Also, invest in bitcoin. Tattoos are bloody expensive!"

James Williams

James Williams is a BA (Hons) English Alumni student of the University of Suffolk who graduated back in 2021. When he's not visiting London or exploring the world of a book, you can find him based in Suffolk where he spends his free time creating artwork, writing, and learning several different languages.

Acknowledgements and Note from Editor

There are many people to thank for this project.

To Dr Lindsey Scott, Dr Darragh Martin, Dr Andrea Smith, Dr Ashley Hickson-Lovence, and Dr Amanda Hodgkinson, many thanks to each of you for your consistent uplifting discussions and support from the conception.

Thank you to Amber Spalding for your assistance in editing *Between These Two Rocks* and *Status*. I appreciate all of your positive comments and advice on these two pieces, and throughout this anthology.

Many thanks to the University of Suffolk, Kate Burgess, the UOS Student Union and The Scarfe Trust for granting the funding that allowed me to successfully print this collection.

A special thanks to Simon James Green and Charles Beal, the president of The Gilbert Baker Foundation, both of which are inspiring people that have dedicated their life and work to supporting the LGBTQ+ community. Thank you for your beautiful words and for reading our anthology, we are extremely grateful for this opportunity.

All the writers that were comfortable enough sharing your work. This anthology would not be what it is without each and every one of you, so thank you and I hope that you are as proud as I am in this anthology.

Lastly, to Laura Ayers, I am immensely grateful for the help that you have given in creating this project. All the work that you have put into this book, the numerous consultations, and your unflinching support. This is us.